Aunt Minnie McGranahan

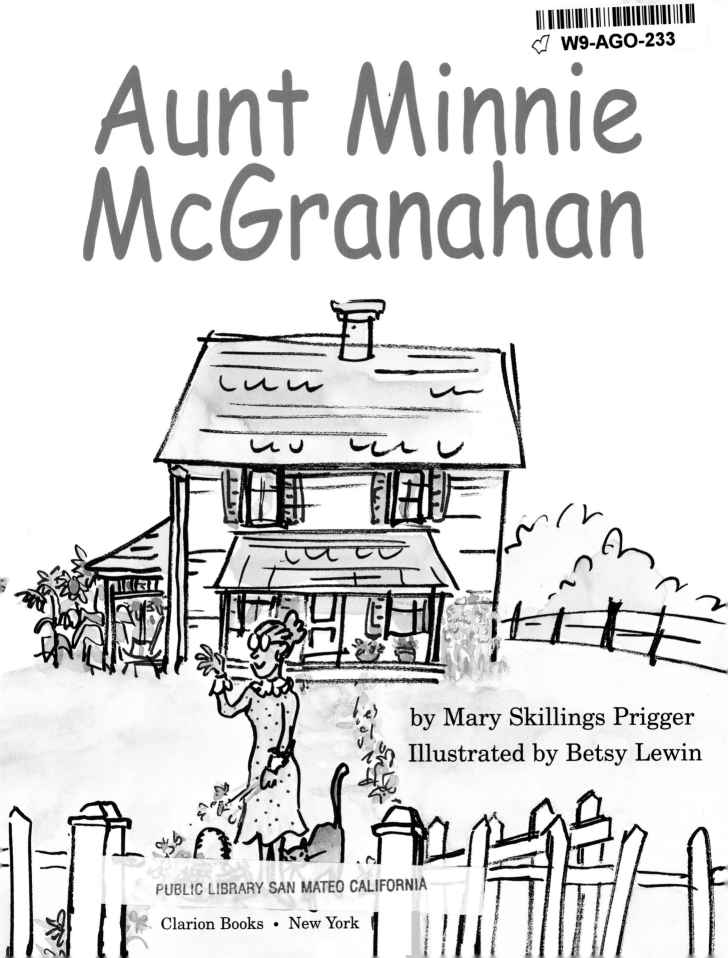

by Mary Skillings Prigger

Illustrated by Betsy Lewin

Clarion Books • New York

Minnie McGranahan had no children.
Minnie was small and tidy
and she always dressed
as though she was ready for company.

She had a neat little house.
She had a neat little garden.
She had a neat little barn
with chickens and cows.
And she had a system.

In Minnie's house, everything happened on a certain day.
She cleaned and washed on Mondays and Thursdays,

she baked and stitched on Tuesdays and Fridays.

And every day she fed the chickens, the cows, and her horse.

"It's lucky Minnie McGranahan has no children.
Children might interfere with Minnie's system,"
agreed the neighbors.

But one day in 1920 a telegram came all the way
from North Dakota to St. Clere, Kansas.
It said:

*"Come quick. Your brother and his wife have had an accident.
Their children are orphans in need of a home."*

The people in the town of St. Clere said,
"What does that Minnie McGranahan know about children?
What ever will she do with them?"
But Minnie paid no attention.
She put on her dress with the lace collar and cuffs
and her white gloves
and took the train from Kansas to North Dakota
to fetch her nieces and nephews.

The oldest was ten and the babies were eight months.
Some of them were triplets.
Some of them were twins.
And some of them were "onlys."
There were nine of them in all—three girls and six boys.
Aunt Minnie brought them all back with her on the train.
Everyone in the town of St. Clere said,
"Nine kids! How will she manage?

Nine kids are more trouble than a litter of kittens."
Aunt Minnie paid no mind.
She was a problem solver and she had a system.
Her system was that—
  The oldest looked after the youngest.
  The ones in the middle looked after each other.
  And Aunt Minnie looked after them all.

She taught them how to stand in line,
how to wait their turn,
and how to help with chores.
Now some of the kids resisted
but Aunt Minnie persisted and—

Some kids were bakers.

Some washed clothes.

Some stitched the quilts.

Some cooked the soup.

Some fed the chickens and gathered eggs
and some hoed the garden.
 The oldest always looked after the youngest.
 The ones in the middle looked after each other.
 And Aunt Minnie looked after them all.

Aunt Minnie had a system for baths.

The oldest lugged buckets from the well
and heated the water.
The middle ones held the towels and mopped the floors.
  The cleanest bathed first.
  The dirtiest bathed last.
  The oldest looked after the youngest.
  And Aunt Minnie checked for dirt.

Aunt Minnie had a system for the johnny house.

It was short and simple.
"Stand in line,
wait your turn,
and help with buttons."

Once a week
Aunt Minnie took her kids to town
in her Model T Ford.
Kids scattered in all directions to run errands.
Aunt Minnie sat behind the wheel with the littlest ones
and waited until they all came back.
  Some brought coffee.
  Some brought fabric.
  Some brought chicken feed.
  And there were candy sticks for all.

Aunt Minnie had a system for keeping her kids neat.

She put stocking tops on their heads
to tame unruly curls.

She cut trousers short to keep them from getting dirty.

She put itchy starched collars on dresses and shirts.

"Well, who would believe it?"
said everybody in the town of St. Clere.
"They look like proper children."

Now sometimes those kids were stubborn,
and sometimes they would fret.
Sometimes they liked to race through chores,
and sometimes they liked to dawdle.
Some of the kids would pout and cry.

But Aunt Minnie used her special system
for getting those chores done.
Her system didn't allow for idleness,
but it did allow for fun.
"Many hands make light work,
and laughing makes it appear lighter," she said.

So there was plenty of laughter
and plenty of noise
mixed into chores.
Aunt Minnie's kids made relay races
of scrubbing the boardwalk.

They juggled with the eggs.

They had target practice with the cornhusks.
They wrestled and they danced

and they worked the farm.

And Aunt Minnie tended to them all.

And of an evening
when chores and supper were done,
Aunt Minnie got out her harmonica.
She played tunes while the kids square-danced and sang
until the little ones fell asleep and were carried off to bed.

In Aunt Minnie's good-night system,
no one had to stand in line for a hug.
  The oldest hugged the youngest.
  The ones in the middle hugged each other.
  And Aunt Minnie hugged them all.

Aunt Minnie kept her kids until they grew up.
One by one they left the neat little house.
But they came back to visit, with their wives
and their husbands and their children.
And they never forgot Aunt Minnie's systems—
especially the hugging system.
Everybody in the town of St. Clere said,
   "Well, who would believe it?
   Minnie McGranahan must have liked children after all."

To Mother, who believed that I could
do anything I set my mind to doing
—M.S.P.

In memory of Dorothy Briley
—B.L.

Clarion Books
a Houghton Mifflin Company imprint
215 Park Avenue South, New York, NY 10003
Text copyright © 1999 by Mary Skilling Prigger
Illustrations copyright © 1999 by Betsy Lewin

Type is 14-point New Century Schoolbook.
Illustrations executed in watercolor.

For information about permission to reproduce selections
from this book, write to Permissions, Houghton Mifflin Company,
215 Park Avenue South, New York, NY 10003.

Printed in Singapore.

Library of Congress Cataloging-in-Publication Data
Prigger, Mary Skillings.
Aunt Minnie McGranahan / by Mary Skillings Prigger ;
illustrated by Betsy Lewin.
p.   cm.
Summary: The townspeople in St. Clere, Kansas, are sure it
will never work out when the neat and orderly spinster,
Minnie McGranahan, takes her nine orphaned nieces and nephews
into her home in 1920.
ISBN 0-395-82270-X
[1. Orderliness—Fiction.   2. Aunts—Fiction. 3. Orphans—Fiction.]
I. Lewin, Betsy, ill.   II. Title.
PZ7.P93534Au   1999
[E]—dc21   98-33501
                                                              CIP
                                                              AC

TWP 10 9 8 7 6 5 4 3 2 1